Classic Pages

Under the Window

窗下

[英]凯特·格林威（Kate Greenaway）著/绘

孔谧 译

向凯特·格林威致敬

辽宁人民出版社

CONTENTS

Under the window is my garden,

Where sweet flower, sweet flowers grow. ···018

Would you be my little wife,

If I ask you? Do! ·· 020

You see, merry Phillis, that dear little maid,

Has invited Belinda to tea. ················· 022

Three tabbies took out their cats to tea,

As well-behaved tabbies as well could be. ······ 026

Little Fanny wears a hat,

Like her ancient Grannie. ···················· 028

目录

窗下是我的花园，
满园芬芳，鲜花盛开。·················· 019

如果我向你求婚，
你愿意嫁给我吗？请一定答应！·················· 021

看，漂亮的小妇人菲利斯，
邀请贝琳达喝下午茶；·················· 023

三个老奶奶带着她们的猫咪喝午茶，
举止优雅又大方。·················· 027

小芬尼戴了一顶帽子，
和奶奶的那顶如出一辙。·················· 029

"Margery Brown, on the top of the hill,

Why are you standing, idle still?" ················· **030**

Little wind, blow on the hill-top,

Little wind, blow down the plain. ······ **034**

Indeed, it is true, it is perfectly true.

Believe me, I am playing no tricks. ··························· **036**

School is over,

Oh, what fun! ···················· **038**

"Little Polly, will you go for a walking today?"

"Indeed, Little Susan, I will if I may." ···················· **040**

As I was walking up the street,

The steeple bells were ringing. ················ **042**

"玛格莉·布朗站在小山上,
你怎么站在这儿啊?痴痴又安静?" 031

微风啊,你吹过山冈,
微风啊,你吹到平原。 035

真的,千真万确,
相信我,我没有胡闹。 037

放学啦,
心情好! 039

"小波莉呀,小波莉,今天去散步吗?"
"小苏珊呀,小苏珊,要是可以,
我一定去!" 041

我漫步在街上,
教堂的钟声响起。 043

Five little sisters walking in a row;

Now, isn't that the best way for little girls to go? ················· 044

In go-cart so tiny,

My sister I drew. ················· 046

Some geese went out for a walking,

To breakfast and to dine. ················· 048

You are going out to tea today,

So mind how you behave. ················· 050

Poor Dick's dead! — The bell we toll,

And lay him in the deep, dark hole. ················· 054

Up you go, shuttlecocks, ever so high!

Why come you down again,

shuttlecocks — why? ················· 056

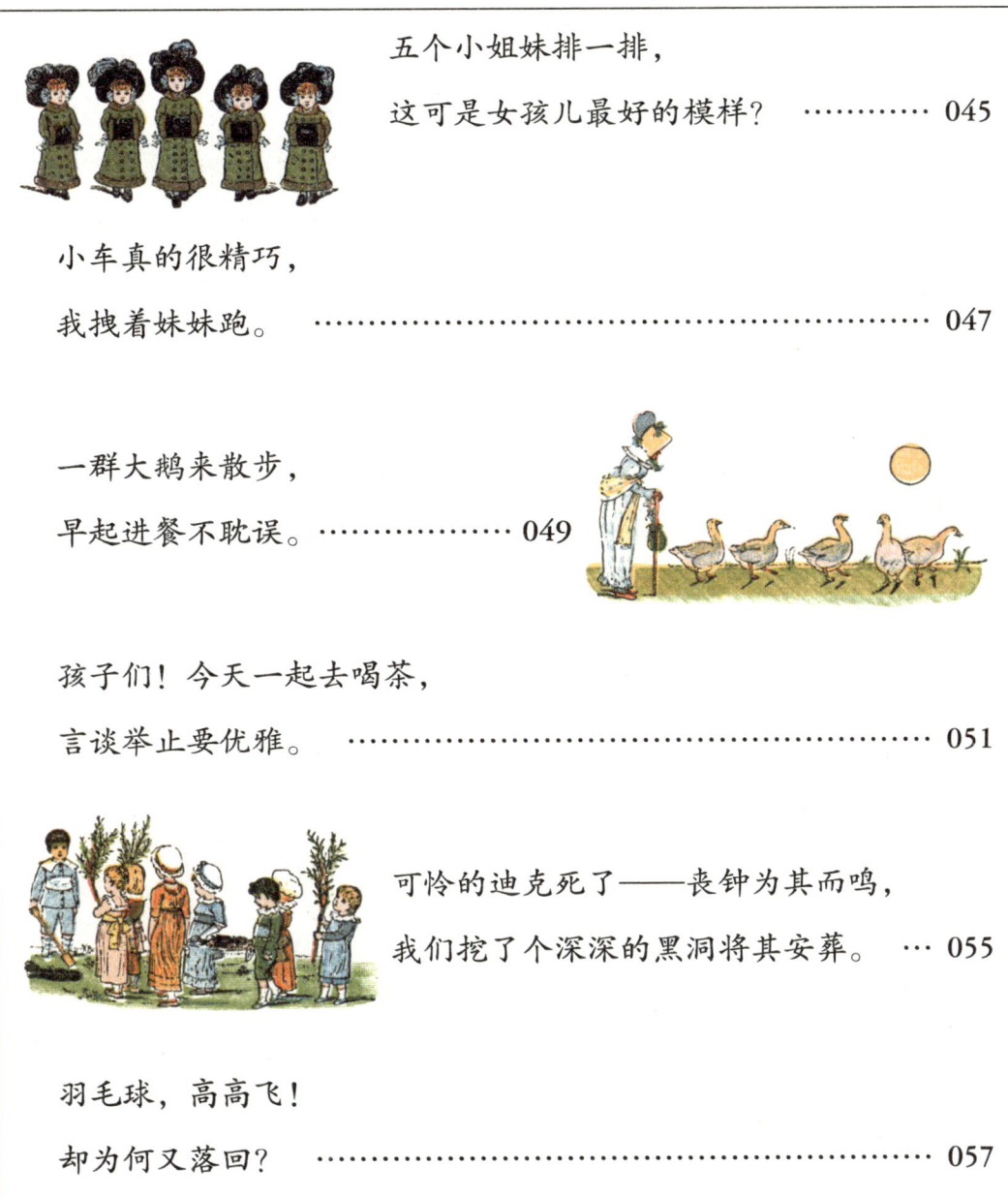

五个小姐妹排一排，
这可是女孩儿最好的模样？ 045

小车真的很精巧，
我拽着妹妹跑。 047

一群大鹅来散步，
早起进餐不耽误。 049

孩子们！今天一起去喝茶，
言谈举止要优雅。 051

可怜的迪克死了——丧钟为其而鸣，
我们挖了个深深的黑洞将其安葬。 ... 055

羽毛球，高高飞！
却为何又落回？ 057

Tommy was a silly boy,

"I can fly," he said. ·················· 058

Higgledy, piggledy! See how they run!

Hopperty, popperty! What is the fun? ······························· 060

Which is the way to Somewhere Town?

Oh, up in the morning early. ················ 064

The boat sails away, like a bird on the wing.

And the little boys dance on the sands in a ring ·············· 066

Pipe thee high, and pipe thee low,

Let the little feet go faster. ············ 068

Polly's, Peg's, and Poppety's

Mamma was kind and good. ······························ 070

汤米是个傻小子，

他嚷着："我会飞！" ………………………………… 059

杂乱无章，为什么人们在乱跑！

乱七八糟，这到底哪里好？ ………………… 061

哪一条是进城的路呀？

哦，记得要早起。 ………………………………… 065

船儿起航啦！像展翅飞翔的鸟儿，

男孩儿围成一圈在沙滩上起舞。 ………… 067

号声高，号声低，

让我们的双脚快舞起。 ………………………… 069

波莉、佩格、波普蒂，

姐仨有个好妈妈。 ………………… 071

Bowl away! Bowl away!

Fast as you can. ················· 074

"For what are you longing, you three little boys?

Oh, what would you like to eat?" ················· 076

O ring the bells! O ring the bells!

We bid you, sirs, good morning. ···080

Then ring the bells! Then ring the bells!

For this fair time of Maying. ·················· 082

I saw a ship that sailed the sea.

It left me as sun went down. ············ 084

Yes, that's the girl that struts about.

She's very proud—so very proud! ················· 086

转哪转,转哪转!

要多快有多快。 ·················· 075

"三个小家伙,你们想来啥?

哦,都想吃点啥?" ············ 077

啊,敲钟啦!啊,敲钟啦!

先生们,早上好! ················ 081

铃铛一摇,铃铛便响!

在这百花盛开的五月。 ······ 083

轮船出海,

夕阳西下。 ························ 085

对,那个昂首阔步的女孩儿

傲慢极了。 ························ 087

It was Tommy who said,

"The sweet spring-time is come." ············ 090

"Shall I sing?" Says the Lark;

"Shall I bloom?" Says the Flower. ············ 092

Little Miss Patty and Master Paul,

Have found two snails on the garden wall. ··· 094

Yes, it is sad of them —

Shocking to me. ································· 096

Now, all of you, give heed unto,

The tale I now relate. ················ 100

What is Tommy running for,

Running for, running for? ···················· 102

是汤米说的，
美好的春光正降临大地。 091

"我能放声歌唱吗？"云雀问。
"我能盛开吗？"花儿问。 093

帕蒂小姐和保罗先生，
在花园的墙上发现两只蜗牛。 095

是的，他们让人难过
让我很吃惊。 097

各位，请注意听，
我要讲个故事。 101

汤米为什么要跑呀？
跑呀跑，跑呀跑？ 103

A butcher's boy met a baker's boy

(It was all of a summer day.) ············ 104

The twelve Miss Pelicoes,

Were twelve sweet little girls. ················· 108

Little baby, if I threw,

This fair blossom down to you. ············ 114

The finest, biggest fish, you see,

Will be the trout that's caught by me. ············ 116

Prince Finikin and his mamma,

Sat sipping their bohea. ········· 118

Heigh ho! —Time creeps but slow;

I've looked up the hill so long. ··············· 122

在这个骄阳似火的夏日，
屠夫的儿子遇到面包师的儿子。 ················· 105

十二位佩利科斯小姐，
是十二个漂亮的小女孩儿。 ················· 109

小宝贝啊，
如果我将盛开的玫瑰抛给你。 ················· 115

瞧！这世界上最肥美、最大的鱼，
是我钓起来的鳟鱼。 ············ 117

菲尼金王子和他的妈妈，
坐在一起喝武夷茶。 ····················· 119

嘿喔，时光渐渐流逝，
我抬眼望山，日子多漫长。 ············ 123

My house's red — a little house;

A happy child am I. ················ 126

Three little girls were sitting on a rail,

Sitting on a rail, sitting on a rail. ·························· 128

Ring the bells — ring!

Hip, hurrah for the King! ··· 132

我住在一栋红色的房子里，
快乐又欢喜。 ………………………………………… 127

三个小姑娘坐在围栏上，
坐在围栏上，坐在围栏上。 …… 129

铃儿响叮当！
为我们的王欢呼又喝彩！ ………………………………… 133

译后记 ……………………………………………………… 134

Under the Window

UNDER the window is my garden,
Where sweet flower, sweet flowers grow;
And in the pear-tree dwells a robin,
The dearest bird I know.

Tho' I peep out bedtimes in the morning,
Still the flowers are up the first;
Then I try and talk to the robin,
And perhaps he'd chat — if he durst.

窗下是我的花园,
满园芬芳,鲜花盛开;
那棵梨树上巢居着一只知更鸟,
它是我的最爱。

清晨早起我探头窗外,
花枝摇曳舒展,
我试着与知更鸟聊天;
它足够勇敢,会与我回应婉转。

WOULD you be my little wife,
If I ask you? Do!
I will buy you such a Sunday frock,
A nice umbrella, too.

And you shall have a little hat,
With such a long white feather,
A pair of gloves, and sandal shoes,
The softest kind of leather.

And you shall have a tiny house,
A beehive full of bees,
A little cow, a largish cat,
And green sage cheese.

如果我向你求婚，
你愿意嫁给我吗？
请一定答应！
我会为你披上婚纱，
配上把可爱的小伞。

你头上那顶帽子，
长长的白羽毛轻盈飞舞，
你戴着手套，穿着凉鞋，
它们都会用最柔软的皮子缝制。

你还会得到一栋小房子，
一蜂巢的蜜蜂，
一头小牛和一只大猫，
还有碧绿鼠尾草做成的奶酪。

YOU see, merry Phillis, that dear little maid,
Has invited Belinda to tea;
Her nice little garden is shaded by trees —
What pleasanter place could there be?

看，漂亮的小妇人菲利斯，
　邀请贝琳达喝下午茶；
　多么美丽的小花园——
　绿树成荫，满园芬芳？

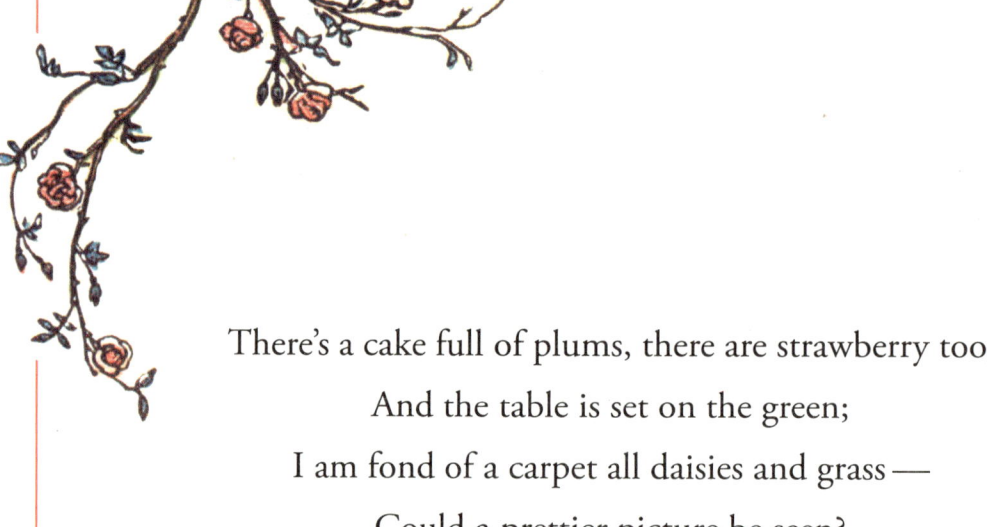

There's a cake full of plums, there are strawberry too,
And the table is set on the green;
I am fond of a carpet all daisies and grass —
Could a prettier picture be seen?

A black bird (yes, blackbird delight in warm weather,)
Is flitting from yonder high spray;
He sees the two little ones talking together —
No wonder the blackbird is gay!

铺满李子蛋糕，还有草莓果盘，
　餐桌就摆在一片绿意之上；
雏菊、碧草的花毯令人心驰神往——
　优美的画卷近在身旁？

暖日中的画眉鸟怡然自得，
　轻盈地掠过，戏水逐浪；
看着小姐妹俩欢声笑语，
　难怪画眉会欢快地飞翔！

THREE tabbies took out their cats to tea,
As well-behaved tabbies as well could be;
Each sat in chair that each preferred,
They mewed for their milk, and they sipped and purred.
Now tell me this (as these cats you've seen them) —
How many lives had these cats between them?

三个老奶奶带着她们的猫咪喝午茶,
举止优雅又大方;
她们坐在各自喜爱的椅子上,
猫咪喵喵叫着喝牛奶,叽里咕噜地撒着欢儿。
看着这些猫咪,请告诉我,
它们中间有几个人?

LITTLE Fanny wears a hat,
Like her ancient Grannie.
Tommy's hoop was (think of that!)
Given him by Fanny.

小芬尼戴了一顶帽子,
和奶奶的那顶如出一辙;
小汤米拿着把铁圈圈,(我想)
正是芬尼给他的玩具。

"MARGERY Brown, on the top of the hill,
Why are you standing, idle still?"
"Oh, I am looking over to London town;
Shall I see the horseman if I go down?"

"玛格莉·布朗站在小山上,
你怎么站在这儿啊?痴痴又安静?"
"哦,我在望着伦敦城啊;
若我现在下山去,能否遇到那位骑士郎?"

"Margery Brown, on the top of the hill,
Why are you standing, listening still?"
"Oh, I hear the bells of London ring.
And I hear the men and the maidens sing."

"Margery Brown, on the top of the hill,
Why are you standing, waiting still?"
"Oh, a knight is there, but I can't go down,
For the bells ring strangely in London town."

"玛格莉·布朗站在小山上,
你怎么站在这儿啊?侧耳倾听什么?
"哦,我在听伦敦城里的铃儿响叮当,
男人们、女人们在欢唱。"

"玛格莉·布朗站在小山上,
你怎么站在这儿啊?静静地等什么?"
"哦,那里有位骑士郎,但我不能下山去,
伦敦城里的铃儿奇怪地叮当响。"

LITTLE wind, blow on the hill-top,
Little wind, blow down the plain;
Little wind, blow up the sunshine,
Little wind, blow off the rain.

微风啊,你吹过山冈,
微风啊,你吹到平原;
微风啊,你驱霾送阳,
微风啊,你吹散细雨。

INDEED, it is true, it is perfectly true.
Believe me, I am playing no tricks;
An old man and his dog bide up there in the moon,
And he's cross as a bundle of sticks.

真的,千真万确,
相信我,我没有胡闹;
一个老头和他的狗藏在月亮里,
他正在变成一捆棍子穿越来人间。

SCHOOL is over,
Oh, what fun!
Lessons finished,
Play begun.

Who will run faster,
You or I?
Who will laugh loudest?
Let us try.

放学啦,
心情好!
下课啦,
玩赛跑!
看看是你,还是我,
谁更快?
过来比比,
谁的笑声最响,谁的笑脸最靓?

"LITTLE Polly, will you go for a walking today?"
"Indeed, little Susan, I will if I may."
"Little Polly, your mother has said you may go;
She was nice to say 'Yes,' she should never say 'No.'"

"A rock has a nest on the top of the tree —
A big ship is coming from the sea,
Now, which would be nicer, the ship or the nest?"
"Why that would be the nicest that Polly like best."

"小波莉呀,小波莉,今天去散步吗?"
"小苏珊呀,小苏珊,要是可以,我一定去!"
"小波莉呀,小波莉,你的妈妈允许你;
　她从不说不呀,每次都同意。"

"树上的石头上建个鸟窝——
　一艘大船从海面驶来,
　哪个最好呢,是大船还是鸟窝?"
"为什么要问哪个是小波莉的最爱。"

AS I was walking up the street,
The steeple bells were ringing;
As I sat down at Mary's feet,
The sweet, sweet bird were singing.

As I walked far into the world,
I met a little fairy;
She plucked this flower, and, as it's sweet,
I've brought it home to Mary.

我漫步在街上,
教堂的钟声响起,
仿佛我坐在玛丽的身旁,
美丽的小鸟在动人地歌唱。

我向世界(森林)深处走去,
遇见位美丽的仙女儿;
她摘下这束向日葵,芬芳美丽;
我会带回家去,送给玛莉。

FIVE little sisters walking in a row;
Now, isn't that the best way for little girls to go?
Each had a round hat, each had a muff,
and each had a new pelisse of soft green stuff.

Five little marigolds standing in a row;
Now, isn't that the best way for marigolds to grow?
Each with a green stalk, and all the five had got
A bright yellow flower, and a new red pot.

五个小姐妹排一排,
这可是女孩儿最好的模样?
顶着圆帽子,戴着皮手笼,
穿着绿皮料的皮外套。

五盆小金盏花排一排,
这可是金盏花最好的模样?
种在红色的花盆里,
绿色的花梗上盛开着金灿灿的花。

IN go-cart so tiny,
My sister I drew;
And I've promised to draw her
The wide world through.

We have not yet started —
I own it with sorrow —
Because our trip's always
put off tomorrow.

小车真的很精巧，
　我拽着妹妹跑。
　我曾经答应她，
　要拉她游世界。

我们至今未启程，
　我也很懊恼——
因为我们的旅行，
总是明日复明日。

SOME geese went out for a walking,
To breakfast and to dine;
They craned their necks, and plumed themselves —
They numbered four from nine;
With their cackle, cackle, cackle!
They thought themselves so fine.

A dame went walking by herself,
A very ancient crone;
She said, "I wish that all you geese
Were starved to skin and bone!
Do stop that cackle, cackle, now,
And leave me here alone."

一群大鹅来散步，
　早起进餐不耽误；
抻着脖，梳着毛——
　九只变四只；
嘎嘎叫起来！
傲娇欢喜好自在。

　一个丑婆婆，
　只身散步烦，
她说："但愿你们这些鹅，
　瘦得皮包骨！
别再嘎嘎地叫人烦，
　让我安静独处。"

YOU are going out to tea today,
So mind how you behave;
Let all accounts I have of you
Be pleasant ones, I crave.

Don't spill your tea, or gnaw our bread,
And don't tease one another;
And Tommy mustn't talk too much,
or quarrel with his brother.

孩子们！今天一起去喝茶，
言谈举止要优雅，
我要看看谁的表现好，
谁是好宝宝。

不要打翻茶具，不要大口嚼面包，
不要互相取笑；
汤米不要口若悬河，
更不要和弟弟争吵。

Say "If you please," and "Thank you, nurse;"
Come home at eight o'clock;
And, Fanny, pray be careful that
You do not tear your frock.

Now, Mind your manners, children five.
Attend to what I say;
And then, perhaps, I'll let you go
Again another day.

"请""谢谢阿姨"挂嘴边,
晚上八点要告辞,
芬尼,请你认真做祷告,
不要拉扯着衣角。

五个宝宝请注意,
一言一行很重要,
记住妈妈说的话,
或许,还会有下次。

POOR Dick's dead! — The bell we toll,
And lay him in the deep, dark hole.
The sun may shine, the clouds may rain,
But Dick will never pipe again!
His quilt will be as sweet as ours —
Bright buttercups and cuckoo flowers.

可怜的迪克死了——丧钟为其而鸣,
我们挖了个深深的黑洞将其安葬,
太阳依然闪耀着光芒,云雨依旧反复无常,
但是迪克再不会展翅歌唱!
金凤花和杜鹃花覆盖在它的身上,
它的被子和我们的一样温暖芬芳。

UP you go, shuttlecocks, ever so high!
Why come you down again, shuttlecocks — why?
When you have got so far, why do you fall?
Where all are high, which is highest of all?

羽毛球，高高飞！
却为何又落回？
羽毛球，远远飞！
却为何又飞回？
高高飞起的球呀，
哪个最难追？

TOMMY was a silly boy,
"I can fly," he said;
He started off, but very soon,
He tumbled on his head.

His little sister Prue was there,
To see how he would do it;
She knew that, after all his boast,
Full dearly Tom would rue it!

汤米是个傻小子,
他嚷着:"我会飞!"
嚷罢就飞快跑起来,
摔个大头朝下。

妹妹蒲璐也在场,
看他如何收场;
她知道汤米每次吹完牛,
准不会有好下场!

HIGGLEDY, piggledy! See how they run!

Hopperty, popperty! What is the fun?

Has the sun or the moon tumbled into the sea?

What is the matter, now? Pray tell it me!

杂乱无章,为什么人们在乱跑!
乱七八糟,这到底哪里好?
是太阳还是月亮掉进了海里?
谁能告诉我这是怎么回事儿。

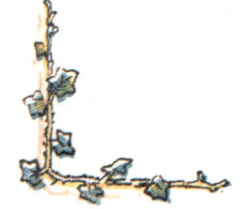

Higgledy, piggledy! How can I tell?
Hopperty, popperty! Hark to the bell!
The rats and the mice even scamper away;
Who can say what may not happen today?

杂乱无章！让我怎么描述？
乱七八糟！像铃声在乱敲！
老鼠、田鼠也在四处乱跑；
谁敢说今天没有什么事儿？

WHICH is the way to Somewhere Town?
Oh, up in the morning early;
Over the tiles and the chimney-pots,
That is the way, quite clearly.

And which is the door to Somewhere Town?
Oh, up in the morning early;
The round red sun is the door to go through,
That is the way, quite clearly.

哪一条是进城的路呀?
哦,记得要早起;
穿过那片瓦房和烟囱,
进城的路啊,就在那里。

哪一扇是通向进城的门呀?
哦,记得要早起;
红红的太阳就是打开进城的门,
进城的路啊,就在那里!

THE boat sails away, like a bird on the wing.
And the little boys dance on the sands in a ring.
The wind may fall, or the wind may rise —
You are foolish to go; you will stay if you're wise.
The little boys dance, and the little girls run;
If it's bad to have money, it's worse to have none.

船儿起航啦!像展翅飞翔的鸟儿,
男孩儿围成一圈在沙滩上起舞,
风会落,风再起——
离开是笨蛋,留下才是机灵鬼,
男孩儿们跳起舞,女孩儿们奔跑嬉戏;
或许有钱并不好,但也好过一无所有的糟。

PIPE thee high, and pipe thee low,
    Let the little feet go faster;
Blow your penny trumpet — blow!
    Well done, little master!

号声高,号声低,
让我们的双脚快舞起;
吹响你的号呀——快吹起!
干得漂亮——小号家!

POLLY'S, Peg's, and Poppety's
Mamma was kind and good;
She gave them each, one happy day,
A little scarf and hood.

波莉、佩格、波普蒂，
姐仨有个好妈妈，
阳光明媚的一天里，
妈妈送每人一条围脖和一顶兜帽。

A bonnet for each girl she bought,
To shield them from the sun;
They wore them in the snow and rain,
And thought it mighty fun.

But sometimes there were naughty boys,
Who called to them at play,
And made this rude remark — "My eye!
Three Grannies out today!"

外加一顶女装帽，遮阳又避雨；
三个姐妹心欢喜，
整天穿戴很整齐，
不管下雪或下雨。

偶遇淘气的男孩子
取乐她们笑嘻嘻，
"快看，快看，来了三个老太婆！"
多么粗鲁又无礼！

BOWL away! Bowl away!
Fast as you can;
He who can fastest bowl,
He is my man!

Up and down, round about —
Don't let it fall;
Ten times, or twenty times,
Beat, beat them all!

转哪转,转哪转!
要多快有多快,
那个滚圈最快的人,
他是我的心上人!

起起落落,摇啊摇,
别让铁圈掉下来。
十圈下来二十圈,
要把对手全打败!

"FOR what are you longing, you three little boys?
Oh, what would you like to eat?"
"We should like some apples, or gingerbread —
Or a fine big drum to beat."

"三个小家伙,你们想来啥?
哦,都想吃点啥?"
"我们想吃苹果或姜饼,
最好还有一面大鼓敲!"

"Oh, what will you give me, you three little boys,
In exchange for these good, good things?"
"Some bread and cheese, and some radishes,
And our little brown bird that sings."

"Now, that won't do, you three little chums.
I'll have something better than that —
Two of your fingers, and two of your thumbs,
In the crown of your largest hat!"

"那你们拿什么换这些好吃的呀，
三个小家伙？"
"拿面包、奶酪和小萝卜，
还有只会唱歌的小棕鸟。"

"那还不够呀，三个好朋友，
我想要更好玩的——
用你们的两根手指和两个大拇指，
伸进最大的帽子做成王冠给我看！"

O ring the bells! O ring the bells!
We bid you, sirs, good morning.
Given thanks, we pray — our flowers are gay,
And fair for your adorning.

O ring the bells! O ring the bells!
Good sirs, accept our greetings:
Where we have been, the woods are green.
So, hey! For our next meeting.

啊，敲钟啦！啊，敲钟啦！
先生们，早上好！
我们感恩，我们祈祷——我们为您送上鲜艳的小花小草，
您一定喜欢没烦恼。

啊，敲钟啦！啊，敲钟啦！
先生们，请接受我们的问候！
我们穿过的森林，树木成荫，青葱碧绿，
嘿，期待再次与您相聚！

THEN ring the bells! Then ring the bells!
For this fair time of Maying;
Our blooms we bring, and while we sing.
O! Hark to what we're saying.

O ring the bells! O ring the bells!
We'll sing a song with any;
And may each year bring you good cheer,
And each of us a penny.

铃铛一摇,铃铛便响!
在这百花盛开的五月;
鲜花怒放,我们歌唱,
哦,我们说过的话还在耳畔回响!

铃铛一摇,铃铛便响!
我们和大家共欢畅,
愿年年各位都快乐,
每个人每年都富足。

I saw a ship that sailed the sea.

It left me as sun went down;

The white birds flew, and followed it

To town — to London town.

Right sad were we to stand alone,

And see it pass so far away;

And yet we know some ship would come —

Some other ship — some other day.

轮船出海,
夕阳西下,
白鸥展翅,
跟去那个伦敦城。

伊人立岸,
观轮远逝,黯然神伤;
虽知某日,
他船将至,他船将至。

YES, that's the girl that struts about.
She's very proud — so very proud!
Her bow-wow's quite as proud as she:
They both are very wrong to be
So proud — so very proud.

对，那个昂首阔步的女孩儿
傲慢极了，
她的狗和她一样，
傲慢极了，
真是不可理喻。

See, Jane and Willy laugh at her.

They say she's very proud!

Says Jane, "My stars! — They're very silly;"

"Indeed they are," cries little Willy,

"To walk so stiff and proud."

瞧,简和威莉在笑话她。

她们说她傲慢至极!

简说:"我的老天——一对傻瓜!"

"就是,就是,"小威莉大声嚷着,

"她们走路的姿态是多么僵硬,如此傲慢至极!"

IT was Tommy who said,
"The sweet spring-time is come;
I see the birds flit,
And I hear the bees hum."

"Oho! Mister Lark,
Up aloft in the sky.
Now, which is the happiest —
Is it you, sir, or I?"

是汤米说的，
美好的春光正降临大地；
我看见鸟儿在飞翔，
我听见蜜蜂在奔忙。

"啊哈，云雀先生，
高高地飞上蓝天。
你，云雀先生还是我——
谁会更欢喜？"

"SHALL I sing?" Says the Lark;
"Shall I bloom?" Says the Flower;
"Shall I come?" Says the Sun;
"Or shall I?" Says the Shower.

Sing your song, pretty Bird;
Roses, bloom for an hour;
Shine on, dearest Sun;
Go away, naughty Shower!

"我能放声歌唱吗?"云雀问。
"我能盛开吗?"花儿问。
"我能普照大地吗?"太阳问。
"我能洒落人间吗?"细雨问。

一展歌喉吧,美丽的小鸟,
尽情地绽放吧,玫瑰花!哪怕如此短暂,
光芒普照吧,亲爱的太阳,
而你,顽皮的细雨,
请快快离开!

LITTLE Miss Patty and Master Paul,
Have found two snails on the garden wall.
"These snails," said Paul, "how slow they walk!
A great deal slower than we can talk.
Make haste, Mr. Snail, travel quicker, I pray;
In a race with our tongues you'd be beaten today."

帕蒂小姐和保罗先生，
在花园的墙上发现两只蜗牛。
"它们爬得太慢啦！"保罗说，
"比我们说话的速度还慢好多。
为你们祈祷啊，蜗牛先生们：
'蜗牛，蜗牛，你们快点走，
超过我们的说话速度算你牛！'"

YES, it is sad of them —
Shocking to me;
Bad — yes, it's bad of them —
Bad of all three.

是的,他们让人难过
让我很吃惊;
坏孩子——是的,都是坏孩子,
三个孩子都很坏。

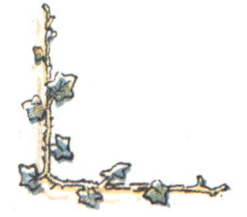

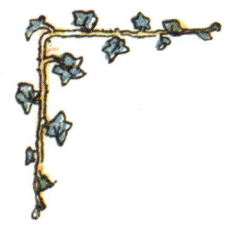
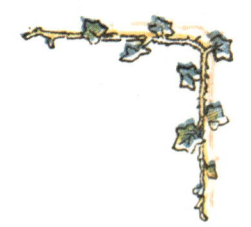

Warnings they've had from me,
Still I repeat them —
Cold is the water —
The fishes will eat them.

Yet they will row about,
Tho' I say "Fie!" to them;
Fathers may scold at it.
Mothers may cry to them.

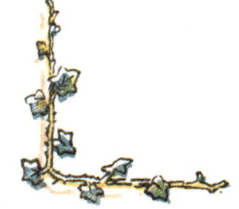

我警告他们

重复地警告着——

河水冰冰凉

鱼会吃掉他们。

但他们还是划船河上游,

我只能说"呸",恨铁不成钢。

父亲们绝对会责备,

母亲们可能会心碎。

NOW, all of you, give heed unto,
The tale I now relate,
About two girls and one small boy,
A cat, and green gate.

A lack! Since I began to speak
(And what I say is true)
It's all gone out of my poor head —
And so goodbye to you!

各位，请注意听，
我要讲个故事，
故事里有两个女孩儿和一个小男孩儿，
一只猫，还有一扇绿色的门。

可是，要讲的时候我什么都想不起来了
（我说的是真的）
大脑顿时一片空白，
只好和大家说拜拜！

WHAT is Tommy running for,
>Running for,
>Running for?
What is Tommy running for,
>On this fine day?

Jimmy will run after Tommy,
>After Tommy,
>After Tommy;
That's what Tommy's running for,
>On this fine day.

汤米为什么要跑呀？
跑呀跑，
跑呀跑？
汤米为什么要跑呀，
这么好的天气里？

吉米在追汤米呀！
追呀追，
追呀追，
汤米才跑呀跑，
哪管天气好不好！

A BUTCHER'S boy met a baker's boy.

(It was all of a summer day.)

Said the butcher's boy to the baker's boy,

"Will you please to walk my way?"

在这个骄阳似火的夏日,
屠夫的儿子遇到面包师的儿子,
他对面包师的儿子说:
"拜托你别挡在我前面!"

Said the butcher's boy to the baker's boy,

"My trade's the best in town."

"If you dare say that," said the baker's boy,

"I shall have to knock you down!"

Said the butcher's boy to the baker's boy,

"That's a wicked thing to do;

And I think, before you've knocked me down,

The cook will blow up you!"

他对面包师的儿子说:
"我家的生意在全镇里首屈一指!"
面包师的儿子说:
"你要再这么说,我绝对会揍扁你!"

屠夫的儿子对面包师的儿子说:
"那可不怎么地!
我想,没等你来打倒我,
厨师先会骂死你!"

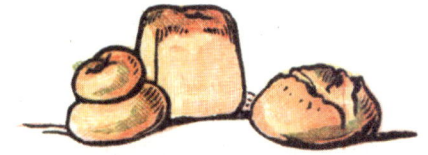

THE twelve Miss Pelicoes,
Were twelve sweet little girls;
Some wore their hair in pigtail plaits,
And some of them wore curls.

The twelve Miss Pelicoes,
Had dinner every day —
A not uncommon thing at all,
You probably will say.

　　十二位佩利科斯小姐，
　是十二个漂亮的小女孩儿，
　　　有的梳辫子，
　　　有的留鬈发。

　　十二位佩利科斯小姐，
　她们每天一起共进晚餐。
　　听到这你会心想，
　不就是平常的一起聚餐？！

The twelve Miss Pelicoes,

Went sometimes for a walk.

It also is a well-known fact,

That all of them could talk.

The twelve Miss Pelicoes,

Of course, to school were sent;

Their parents wished them to excel,

In each accomplishment.

The twelve Miss Pelicoes,

Played music — *Fal-la-la!*

Which consequently made them all,

The pride of their papa.

The twelve Miss Pelicoes,

Learned dancing and the globes;

Which proves that they were wise,

And had that patience which was Job's.

十二位佩利科斯小姐，
有时会一起出门散步，
大家知道，她们无所不谈，
聊起天南和地北，说天也说地。

十二位佩利科斯小姐，
背着书包上学去；
父母希望她们卓尔不群，
成绩优异数第一。

十二位佩利科斯小姐，
伴着"发啦啦"的小旋律；
一直是爸爸的骄傲，
优秀又争气！

十二位佩利科斯小姐，
学习去跳圆圈舞；
证明自己聪明有灵气，
还有约伯的耐心好脾气。

The twelve Miss Pelicoes,

were always most polite —

Said "if you please," and "Many thanks,"

"Good morning," and "Good night."

The twelve Miss Pelicoes,

You plainty see, were taught,

To do things they didn't like,

which means, the things they ought.

Now, farewell, Miss Pelicoes,

I wish ye a good day —

About these twelve Miss Pelicoes

I've nothing more to say.

十二位佩利科斯小姐，
总是彬彬有礼；
"请"和"多谢"，
"早安"与"晚安"！

十二位佩利科斯小姐，
要知道，她们学习的东西她们并不喜欢
她们只是在学她们应该做的
一件一件。

那么，再见吧，女士们！
日安！
关于这十二个女孩儿的故事
我也不想再唠叨得令你烦！

LITTLE baby, if I threw,
This fair blossom down to you,
Would you catch it as you stand,
Holding up each tiny hand,
Looking out of those grey eyes,
Where such deep, deep wonder lies?

小宝贝啊,
如果我将盛开的玫瑰抛给你,
你能否站在原地将它接起,
举起你的小手来,
睁大灰色的双眼,
看看是否有奇迹?

THE finest, biggest fish, you see,
Will be the trout that's caught by me;
But if the monster will not bite,
Why, then I'll hook a little mite.

瞧！这世界上最肥美、最大的鱼，
是我钓起来的鳟鱼；
但如果这大家伙不上钩，
我就继续钓些小家伙。

PRINCE Finikin and his mamma,
Sat sipping their bohea;
"Good gracious!" Said his Highness, "why,
What girl is this I see?"

菲尼金王子和他的妈妈，
坐在一起喝武夷茶，
"我的天哪！"王子惊叹道：
"快看这个女孩是谁，好美丽！"

"Most certainly it cannot be,
A native of our town;"
And he turned him round to his mamma,
Who set her teacup down.

But Dolly simply looked at them,
She did not speak a word;
"She has no voice!" Said Finikin;
"It's really quite absurd."

Then Finikin's mamma observed,
"Dear Prince, it seems to me,
She looks as if she'd like to drink,
A cup of my bohea."

So Finikin poured out her tea,
And gave her currant-pie;
Then Finikin said, "dear mamma,
What a kind Prince am I!"

"我敢肯定她不是
我们镇上的居民,"
王子转头望向妈妈。
母后放下手里那杯茶。

可多莉平静地看着他们,
没说一句话。
"她怎么不说话?"菲尼金王子问。
"这个女孩好奇怪!"

菲尼金王子的妈妈仔细看了看,
"亲爱的王子,在我看来,
她只想喝杯
武夷茶!"

于是,菲尼金王子倒了杯茶,
还送给小女孩儿醋栗派。
"亲爱的妈妈,
我这个王子可不赖!"

HEIGH ho! — Time creeps but slow;

I've looked up the hill so long;

None come this way, the sun sinks low,

And my shadow's very long.

嘿喔，时光渐渐流逝，
我抬眼望山，日子多漫长；
夕阳西下，无人来往。
只有我形单影只，寂寥悠长。

They said I should sail in a little boat,
Up the stream, by the great white mill;
But I've waited all day, and none come my way;
I've waited — I'm waiting still.

They said I should see a fairy town,
With houses all of gold,
And silver people, and a gold church steeple —
But it wasn't the truth they told.

有人说我应独撑一叶小舟,
顺流而上,停靠在那白色磨坊,
我却等了一天不见来路踪影,
只有我形单影只,寂寥神伤。

有人说我应该去看看那座神奇之城,
有金子盖的屋房,
银色般的人群和金光闪闪的教堂,
但我知道他们说的并非真相。

MY house's red — a little house;
A happy child am I.
I laugh and play the livelong day;
I hardly ever cry.

I have a tree, a green, green tree,
To shade me from the sun;
And under it I often sit,
When all my work is done.

My little basket I will take,
And trip into the town;
When next I'm there I'll buy some cake,
And spend my bright half-crown.

我住在一栋红色的房子里,
快乐又欢喜。
整日笑声朗朗,无忧又无虑。
更没人见我哭泣。

我有棵小树,青葱又碧绿。
为我遮阴蔽雨,
我常常坐在树下,
做完我全部的工作毫无倦意。

我也提着小篮子,
偶尔溜达进城去,
买了蛋糕,花了半克朗,
日子过得清新而惬意!

THREE little girls were sitting on a rail,
Sitting on a rail,
Sitting on a rail;
Three little girls were sitting on a rail,
On a fine hot day in September.

三个小姑娘坐在围栏上,
　　坐在围栏上,
　　坐在围栏上;
九月的天气多晴朗,
三个小姑娘坐在围栏上。

What did they talk about that fine day,

That fine day,

That fine day?

What did they talk about that fine day —

That fine hot day in September?

The crows and the corn they talked about,

Talked about,

Talked about;

But nobody knows what was said by the crows,

On that fine hot day in September.

她们如何谈这美好的天?
　　美好的一天。
　　美好的一天?
她们如何谈这美好的天,
　　在这九月的热天里?

她们在谈乌鸦和玉米,
　　　谈呀谈,
　　　谈呀谈;
但是没人知道乌鸦都说了什么,
　　在这九月的热天里。

RING the bells — ring!

Hip, Hurrah for the King!

The dunce fell into the pool, oh!

The dunce was going to school, oh!

The groom and the cook,

Finished him out with a hook,

And he piped his eye like a fool, oh!

铃儿响叮当!
为我们的王欢呼又喝彩!
哦!笨孩子落池塘,
哦!笨孩子上学堂。
马夫和厨师合力
用鱼钩将他钓起,
让他的眼睛瞪得像傻瓜,哦!

译后记

童心未泯的绘本创作者

凯特·格林威（Kate Greenaway，1846—1901），是英国19世纪最具影响力的童书插画家之一，甚至与创作《青蛙求偶记》（*A Frog He Would A-Wooing Go*）的蓝道夫·凯迪克（Randolph Caldecott）、绘制《睡美人》（*The Sleeping Beauty*）的沃尔特·克莱恩（Walter Crane）并称为"英国绘本三巨头"，他们三人大大地改变了现代图画书的表现形式，更引领了英国绘本的黄金发展时期。

凯特·格林威

成长于英国乡村的纯真之心

1846年,凯特·格林威出生于伦敦的霍克斯顿区(Hoxton)。因为父亲是一名绘图员和雕版印刷师,当格林威刚学会握笔的时候,父亲就鼓励她开始画画。稍长之后的格林威除了画画之外,也非常喜欢装饰自己的洋娃娃,年纪小小就展现出她对艺术的喜爱。12岁时,她进入皇家女子艺术学校(Royal Female School of Art)学习装饰艺术;之后就读于希瑟利艺术学校(Heatherley School of Fine Art),并在22岁时举办了她人生中的第一场水彩画展。

16岁的凯特·格林威

格林威在一个叫做罗雷斯顿(Rolleston)的小村庄度过了其童年的大段时光,她曾经说过:"当我还是个孩子时,在乡间度过了非常快乐的时光。"乡村的老式英国风情和童年的愉快记忆对她的绘画风格产生了很大的影响,从她的作品中可以发现,画作里充满了浪漫的氛围,场景大多在田野、花园、牧场或是小村庄,

凯特·格林威的服装设计风格

笔下的人物则以女性和孩童为主。仔细评析格林威的画作可以发现，她强调细节，用色鲜明强烈，有其独特的纤细之美。

19世纪末的格林威风潮

19世纪70年代，英国有一位知名的木刻印刷师埃德蒙·埃文斯（Edmund Evans），他改善了彩色印刷的技术，大大提升了原本低劣的图画书品质，同时他也不断地挖掘优秀的插画家，并一同合作，共同出版图画书。格林威原本专为节庆贺卡绘制插图，埃文斯相中了她的风格，认为十分符合当时维多利亚时代的大众口味，便邀请她创作了格林威人生的第一本图画书——《窗下》（Under the Window）。

埃文斯曾说，当他一读完《窗下》的诗文和插图草稿之后，便深深为之着迷，于是他马上说服出版商出版此书，在首印时就大手笔地印了两万本，这在当时是相当庞大的印量。不过读者的反应证明了埃文斯的眼光没错，《窗下》果然大受欢迎，上市后便售罄，后足足加印了五万本。前前后后更再版多次，于格林威一生当中，总共销售超过十万本，相继翻译成德文、法文、日文等多国语言，着实成为时代经典。

因为《窗下》在商业上的成功，插画中的人物穿着常被人拿

凯特·格林威故居，位于英国伦敦汉普斯特德，由英国著名建筑师理查德·肖设计建造

来讨论研究。格林威笔下人物的服饰参照了18世纪末至19世纪初的穿着风格，虽然在格林威生活的19世纪末，这种风格被认为有些过时，但19世纪下半叶正处于欧洲的艺术服饰运动（Artistic Dress Movement）时期，主张拒绝高度复杂僵硬的穿衣风格，兴起使用更为简洁的设计；同时也受到前拉斐尔派的艺术风格影响，让格林威笔下的服饰重新流行起来。因此，格林威成了一个家喻户晓的名字，甚至在当时掀起了一股格林威风潮（Greenaway Vogue）。

与同时期崭露头角的凯迪克即克莱恩相比较，格林威的作品从女性视角出发，风格较为细腻优美，她笔下的人物穿着18世纪后期流行的服饰，例如镶有花边的礼袍、头上和腰间都系着丝带；文字更多着眼于美好纯真的时光，关注孩子的天真烂漫、纯真朴实的心灵，与同时期的其他两位插画家有着明显不同的风格。

余音绕梁的经典

格林威大部分作品的文字都来自民间耳熟能详的歌谣，例如《鹅妈妈童谣》（*Mother Goose*）、《金盏花花园》（*Marigold Garden*）、《小安》（*Little Ann*）、《四月儿歌》（*April Baby's Book of Tunes*）、《儿童生日书》（*Kate Greenaway's Birthday Book for Children*）以及《苹果派》（*Apple Pie*）皆是以童谣作为改编而成。

1855年，为了纪念格林威对插画领域的贡献，英国图书馆协会（The Library Association）以她的名字创办了"凯特·格林威奖"（The CILIP Kate Greenaway Medal），此奖是英国历史最悠久并且最重要的绘本奖项，评选标准包含了艺术风格、格式、图文整合与视觉印象，对于插画的严格审视，让格林威奖在国际上有着极高的声誉，至今仍是许多插画家、作家角逐的绘本大奖。

无数英国孩子是在格林威插画的童书陪伴下长大的，有些甚至受到她的绘画风格影响，成为著名的插画家。即使一百多年过去了，格林威的作品依然为全世界的读者喜爱着，每一次翻阅都能碰上可爱的孩子与风景，感受属于那个时代的艺术氛围，相信不论是大人还是孩子，都可以在这些经典图画书中获得美感和乐趣。

图书在版编目（CIP）数据

窗下：英汉对照 /（英）凯特·格林威（Kate Greenaway）著绘；孔谧译. —沈阳：辽宁人民出版社，2024.7

（"世界儿童经典插图版"丛书）
ISBN 978-7-205-10827-4

Ⅰ.①窗… Ⅱ.①凯… ②孔… Ⅲ.①儿童故事—图画故事—英国—现代 Ⅳ.①I561.85

中国国家版本馆 CIP 数据核字（2023）第 156870 号

出版发行：辽宁人民出版社
地　址：沈阳市和平区十一纬路 25 号　邮编：110003
电　话：024-23284321（邮　购）　024-23284324（发行部）
传　真：024-23284191（发行部）　024-23284304（办公室）
http://www.lnpph.com.cn

| 印　　　刷：辽宁新华印务有限公司
| 幅面尺寸：180mm × 210mm
| 印　　张：6
| 字　　数：68千字
| 出版时间：2024 年 7 月第 1 版
| 印刷时间：2024 年 7 月第 1 次印刷
| 责任编辑：阎伟萍　孙　雯
| 装帧设计：留白文化
| 责任校对：耿　珺
| 书　　号：ISBN 978-7-205-10827-4
| 定　　价：66.00元